Published in North America in 2013 by Owlkids Books Inc.

Published in France under the title *Merci, le vent!* © 2011
Éditions Milan, 300, rue Léon-Joulin, 31101 Toulouse Cedex 9
www.editionsmilan.com

Translation © 2012 Sarah Quinn

Owlkids Books acknowledges the financial support of the Canada
Council for the Arts, the Ontario Arts Council, the Government of
Canada through the Canada Book Fund (CBF) and the Government of
Ontario through the Ontario Media Development Corporation's Book
Initiative for our publishing activities.

Published in Canada by   Published in the United States by
Owlkids Books Inc.   Owlkids Books Inc.
10 Lower Spadina Avenue   1700 Fourth Street
Toronto, ON M5V 2Z2   Berkeley, CA 94710

Library and Archives Canada Cataloguing in Publication

Manceau, Édouard, 1969-
    Windblown / written and illustrated by Édouard Manceau.

Translation of: Merci, le vent!
ISBN 978-1-926973-77-7

    I. Title.

PZ7.M333Wi 2013   j843'.92   C2012-904871-2

Library of Congress Control Number: 2012945653

Manufactured in Dongguan, China, in May 2013, by Toppan Leefung
Packaging & Printing (Dongguan) Co., Ltd.
Job #BAYDC2/R1

B   C   D   E   F   G

 Publisher of Chirp, chickaDEE and OWL
www.owlkidsbooks.com

"Riches consist more in use
than in possession."
—Aristotle

With thanks to Dominique Rateau, who
has learned exactly how to read me, and to
Patrick "Tic-Tic" Ben Soussan for the great
time we shared in Toulouse
during the Journées Spirale.

For Olivier de Rivaz

Windblown

Édouard Manceau

Translated by Sarah Quinn

Owl kids

One tiny scrap of paper . . .

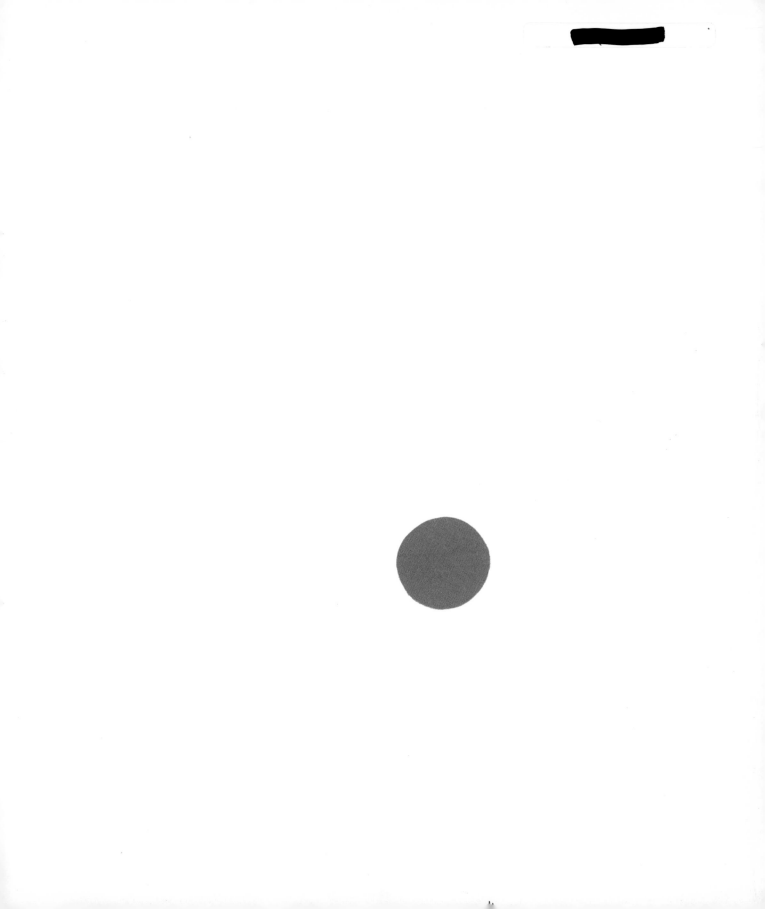

Look, there's another!

Now there are three!

And now there are even more . . .

Where did they come from?

Whose are they?

"They're mine!" said the chicken.
"I saw them lying around!"

"No, they're mine!" replied the fish.
"I'm the one who cut the paper into the pieces
that the chicken saw lying around."

"No, no, they're mine!" chirped the bird.
"I'm the one who made the paper
that the fish cut into the pieces
that the chicken saw lying around."

"No, no, no, they're mine," whispered the snail.
"I'm the one who shaped the wood
that the bird made into paper
that the fish cut into the pieces
that the chicken saw lying around."

"No, no, no, no, they're mine!" croaked the frog.
"I'm the one who found the tree,
shaped by the snail,
that the bird made into paper
that the fish cut into the pieces
that the chicken saw lying around."

"Shhh . . . " said the wind.
"*I* blew and blew as hard as I might.
I toppled the tree found by the frog,
shaped by the snail,
that the bird made into paper
that the fish cut into the pieces
that the chicken saw lying around."

"And I'll blow and blow as hard as I can until all the tiny scraps are high in the air."

"And with one last gust,
I'll blow them over to you."

They're yours now too.
What will *you* do?